THE NARROW VIEW

By Bazzel Baz

ILLUSTRATIONS
By Ken Dutton

Published by Pen, Cloak, & Dagger Inc.
Manhattan Beach, CA 90266
United States of America

eBook ISBN 978-1-949280-00-5
Paperback ISBN 978-1-949280-01-2
Hardback ISBN 978-1-949280-02-9

Printed in the United States

Once upon a time there was a village of people who lived in a very uncomfortable world. As long as they could remember from the time of their childhood it had always been that way

The sun was hot, the land was dry and there was only one very narrow tree to provide shade.

The tree was so narrow and so small that the one leaf it had on its branches could only provide enough shade for one villager at a time and for only one part of their body at a time. Can you imagine how uncomfortable they must have been?

The people of the village would take turns sitting under the very narrow tree. Sometimes they would stick a toe under the one leaf of the tree for shade, sometimes a hand, sometimes a part of their head and sometimes just their nose.

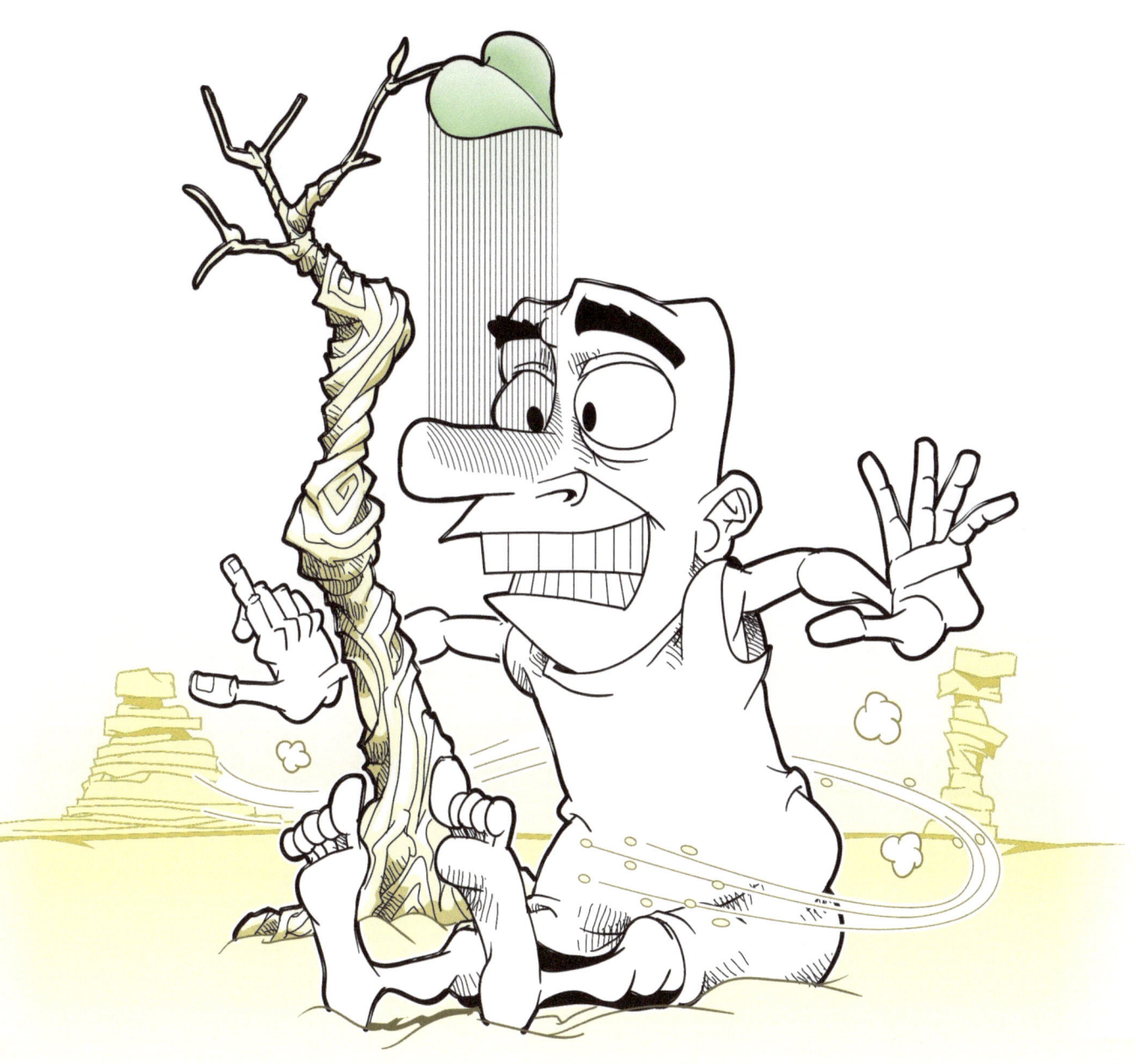

But inevitably the rest of their body would get sun burned which made life that much more uncomfortable.

And so the people of the village remained uncomfortable day in and day out because it was the only thing they knew to do, the very thing they had grown accustomed to...their very narrow view.

Then one night a great wind blew from the North.

It blew so hard that it swept all the people of the village up in the air and carried them hundreds of miles away from their uncomfortable world.

The great wind gently laid them down in front of the biggest tree they had ever seen. It was enormous... as towering a giant of a Red Wood that had ever been created.

All the people of the village just stood there looking up, amazed at their discovery, not really knowing what to do except stand there and be amazed. Some were overwhelmed, some were scared and others simply smiled.

As the sun began to creep into the sky, the people of the village were at a loss as to where to stand, or sit or lie.

But, as the giant Red Wood would have it, its branches provided shade for every person in the village for every part of their body. It was in fact the most amazing thing they had ever experienced... and they were happy.

Indeed, this was a tree that had stood the test of time, was wise and could teach the people of the village many wonderful things. When the sun would shift, the tree would guide the people to the shade of its other branches. When it would rain, the tree would do the same.

The moisture from its trunk took away the dryness of the day and the roots like big, strong arms, offered warmth for the night so that all the people of the village felt secure enough to nestle in between them, close their eyes and go to sleep.

Each morning when they would wake they would hug the giant Red Wood tree and say, "Oh how I love you so much... thank you, thank you, thank you."

Others would say, "I want to spend the rest of my life with this tree."

And others would say, "This is what I have always hoped for... the one thing I never had."

It was a perfect world, a protected world, a world they had always dreamed of, a comfortable world... and the people of the village were happy... until one day.

Something familiar began to stir inside their inner being. They weren't sure exactly what it was, and they really didn't like the way it felt, but it was familiar.

So they all gathered in the shade and comfort of the giant Red Wood tree, looking up at all its beauty and strength and began to make excuses.

"I don't deserve the comfort of this tree," said one.

"I don't have time to enjoy the comfort of this tree," said another.

"Now that I've really taken the time, it doesn't look like I expected it to look," said another.

"I want more shade... there can never be enough," said another.

"I'm afraid that I will be disappointed," said another.

"I'm afraid that I might get hurt if I try and enjoy the fun of climbing on its branches," said another.

"I don't want to let my guard down because people who do that are vulnerable, exposed and open to the unknown," said another.

"I'm strong and self sufficient...I don't need anything from anyone, especially this tree," said another.

"Been there, done that, and it's nothing to write home about," said another.

"It's easier to be under a smaller tree that doesn't have so many options... where I can be alone," said another.

"All good things come to an end, so why even start?" said another.

"My life was just fine the way it was," said another.

"I like being able to do what I want, when I want, how I want, and this tree is too big to control," said another.

"I don't want someone telling me what to do," said another.

"What's in it for me?" said another.

And so the people stood there looking at the giant Red Wood tree and then looking at one another as the frustration of the unknown but very familiar feeling welled up inside each of them. And soon the frustration turned to anger and soon the anger turned to action.

All the people of the village began chipping away at the bark of the tree and then the roots and then the trunk until finally... the giant Red Wood tree with its branches that provided shade for every person in the village for every part of their body, the very tree that once was the most amazing thing they had ever experienced... the thing that made them happy, came crashing helplessly down to the ground.

They all turned and walked away and returned to live in a very uncomfortable world saying to one another that, as long as they could remember from the time of their childhood it had always been that way.

The sun was hot, the land was dry and there was only one very narrow tree to provide shade.

The tree was so narrow and so small that the one leaf it had on its branches could only provide enough shade for one villager at a time and for only one part of their body at a time. Can you imagine how uncomfortable they must have been?

Once again, the people of the village would take turns sitting under the very narrow tree. Sometimes they would stick a toe under the one leaf of the tree for shade, sometimes a hand, sometimes a part of their head and sometimes just their nose.

But inevitably the rest of their body would get sun burned which made life that much more uncomfortable.

And so the people of the village remained uncomfortable day in and day out because it was the only thing they knew to do, the very thing they had grown accustomed to... their very narrow view.

THE END